# The Price of Doing Business IN MEXICO

# The Price of Doing Business in MEXICO

## poems by
## BOBBY BYRD

*The Price of Doing Business in Mexico.*
Copyright ©1998 by Bobby Byrd.

FIRST EDITION

**Library of Congress Cataloging-in-Publication Data**

Byrd, Bobby, 1942-
 The price of doing business in Mexico and other poems / by
Bobby Byrd. – 1st ed.
  I.   cm.
   ISBN 0-938317-40-7 (paper)
 II.  Title.
PS3552.Y66P75   1998
811'.54—dc21

                                         98-27011
                                          CIP

*Cover image © Virgil Hancock, 1996*
*Drawing "The Price of Doing Business in Mexico"*
*© David Nakabayashi, 1998*
*Photo of man in* ghilli *suit © James Evans, 1997*
*Photo "Byrd in Red Hat" © Richard Baron, 1998*
*Cover and Book Design by Vicki Trego Hill of El Paso*
*Printed in Canada by Transcontinental Printing*

# Contents

꙰ My mother, Charlotte Stanage Byrd Grider, died on November 18, 1997. She was 84 years old. My father, William Hudson Byrd, died on June 13, 1945. He was 33. I was just barely three years when he died, so I don't remember him. I do know this—sometime in August (maybe it was late July) 1941, my mother and father made love, a hot and humid night in Clarksdale, Mississippi, perfectly white sheets, the screened windows open to catch what little breeze moved through those huge dark trees. I was conceived then, the completion of that trinity.

This book is for them, for my mother and father, with love and thanks for what they gave me.

*And always for Lee.*

"GOD AIN'T NOWHERE NEAR HERE, child," Socrates' aunt, Bellandra Beaufort, used to say.

"He's a million miles away; out in the middle'a the ocean somewhere. An' he ain't white like they say he is neither."

"God's black?" little Socrates asked the tall, skinny woman. He was sitting in her lap, leaning against her bony breast.

"Naw, baby," she said sadly. "He ain't black. If he was, there wouldn't be all this mess down here wit' us. Naw. God's blue."

"Blue?"

"Uh-huh. Blue like the ocean. Blue. Sad and cold and far away like the sky is far and blue. You got to go a long long way to get to God. And even if you get there he might not say a thing. Not a damn thing."

~ from Walter Mosley's
*Always Outnumbered, Always Outgunned*

––––––

DREAMS are an important source of ideas for me, as much as the real world. I remember something Norman Mailer wrote about. The medicine man in some unheard of tribe doesn't consider himself a mystic, he considers himself a realist. I think that God, in the same way, considers himself a realist, and that we are realists when we dream.

~ MARK O'BRIEN in an interview
in *Poetry Flash*, April 1998

## Steak and Eggs—A Prologue

Fifty three years ago my father
sat at the kitchen table
and ate steak and eggs for breakfast.
He drank coffee with real cream.
The world was at war,
men killing each other as fast as they could
to feed the hungry moon.
My father sliced off a piece of steak
and with his fork
rubbed it into the gooey egg yolk.
He picked up the newspaper
and read about the number of
dead men whose souls
had slipped into the emptiness.
My mother washed the dishes
and waited
with the four of us children
for my father
to make the same journey.
It was an accident, the Army said,
the way his plane
tumbled
into the Mississippi earth.
I have never forgiven my father
for leaving me like that,

although I have spent
the last 20 years trying.
This morning I am eating steak and eggs.
It is a beautiful November morning,
five Inca doves cooing on the front lawn.
I have a granddaughter now.
She is one month old.
Her name is Hannah.

# The Price of Doing Business in Mexico

If you want to know my story,
then you got to buy me a drink.
$\qquad\qquad\qquad$ Tequila
with the blue horseshoe,
a cold Bohemia for a chaser, okay?
Call that waiter over here,
the one with the beard and the brown eyes.
His name is Moisés.
He's my friend.
I hate this place,
but I stick around because of him.

Ah, that's better.
Thanks.
Now just sit back and listen.

My name is Andre Bollaert.
I'm a private dick out of El Paso, Texas.
My specialty is Mexico,
and these days business is good.
Rich folks too scared to find out for themselves
send me down here
to find out the real skinny
of what's going on.
I've made good money
rummaging around in the dark alleys
that lead directly from the souls of

Carlos Salinas and his brujo brother Raúl.
I was the first gringo
who found those ominous mushrooms
in the stink
and dregs of rotting lucre, the
dangerous spores
drifting toward the 21st Century.
Some goon following orders
decreed from the Aztec Void
dragged the porous

                    obstinate

                    cadaver

of Luis Donaldo Colosio
thru that same confusion.
Pop-eyed Zedillo with

                    the long

                    sad

                    face

came crawling to pull up the rear
in the wake of that aboriginal mystery.
His PhD from Harvard surely didn't
solve the emptiness in his heart.

                    *But then is not now.*
                    *It never has been.*

An old hag selling newspapers
on a nowhere corner in DF told me that once.
Tell your own story, she said.

Which begins here with a fat registered letter.
Inside the envelope was a $5,000 retainer,

two credit cards in my name,
a plane ticket
and a ticket for a first class bus
that would take me those last 60 miles
from the swamps of DF
and land me here in fucking Toluca.
My client was an art collector,
a foolish rich woman from a place like Omaha
who once vomited up enough peyote buttons
to change her life forever.
Even the ants chewing on a chocolate chip cookie
became God
in the bleak corners of her soul.
Professional principles refuse to let me say more.
Her letter told me to check into
this god-forsaken Hotel San Francisco
and wait to be contacted.
My child support payment was due,
I had some cheese and stale bread in the refrigerator,
two small tubs of strawberry yogurt,
and three lonely bottles of ice cold Bohemia.
So I did what the letter said.


The old Mexican Gods with the unpronounceable names
have never forgiven cities like Toluca.
This city drips
with the shitty karma that the Spanish left behind.
This putrid Hotel San Francisco is proof of that pudding.
It's a lousy place,
overpriced Mexican-modern smelling
like disinfectant

and waiting to fall apart.
When I first walked in,
the desk clerk was picking his nose and watching a telenovela
which said only rich people have interesting lives.
Organ music was being piped in from Salt Lake City.
I certainly didn't need the music.
Beethoven scares me.
I took the glass elevator up to my room,
number 717.
I hoped the numbers would make my luck good.

At least the room had a window.
But the rain and thick clouds
didn't help the feeling
that had begun to creep over me—
I wish I hadn't come to Toluca.
Out over the ugly rooftops
green mountains rose up in the north
like promises,
but I was too tired to worry what the promises were.
The best thing to do was to hang out in my room
and watch the telly, practice
my slow-assed gabacho Spanish.
I found an old-fashioned western
where they had a Mexican for a bad guy.
His name was Pancho,
and Pancho murdered four white men
before I had a chance to take my pants off,
pour myself a brandy and climb into bed.
Just before Pancho was going to rape
a peroxide blonde (Doris Day

hablando the Spanish)
the sheriff
caught Pancho. He hung
the poor Mexican bastard from the neck,
Pancho swinging out there
in the imitation cold desert darkness,
his boots jerking
a little death dance
until he was completely
dead
somewhere near
the holy city of Las Vegas, Nevada.
I fell asleep.

That evening started hungry and sad.
I knew that somewhere in Toluca thousands
of men and women
were putting together
Ford automobiles and trucks.
Their labor made the air taste bad.
This restaurant here was closed.
The waiter,
who was also the Tuesday night cook,
hadn't shown up for work.
His name was Odilón.
Instead of going to work,
Odilón had bought a bottle of tequila,
six caguamas of Corona,
a sackful of limes,
then jumped into a taxi rojo.
The taxi had been circling

the hotel for two hours waiting for me.
The nose-picking asshole at the front desk
told me this, told me to wait by the front door, told me
to look for the taxi rojo, told me
not to carry my gun.
I asked him how did he know that I had a gun.
He said: Gringos worry too much.

The lousy Toluca rain was still drizzling.
I waved at the first taxi rojo that turned the corner.
A skinny guy riding shotgun,
the black bowtie and white jacket of a waiter,
said, Yes, his name was Odilón, said
his job was to save at least one gringo in his life.
He told me to jump in.
The taxi driver was a big guy with a bull-like head.
I asked Odilón what the guy's name was,
but Odilón said not to worry,
that taxi drivers in Toluca refuse to have names.
They only have numbers.
This guy with the bull's head was Number 3.
Like in the way God sometimes visits,
Odilón said with a wily smile that jingled of broken teeth.

Huh? I said.

The taxi dashed through the lights of Toluca's poverty
into the darkness, pointing
toward the green mountains I had seen from my window.
I wondered out loud where the rich people lived.
The nameless bull-headed taxi driver Number 3
said he didn't know, said he didn't care.

His unerring English scared me.
He said that civilization,
whatever that is,
was slipping away through my dark window.

We traveled for what seemed hours
cocooned in that taxi rojo, sipping
at various combinations of tequila and beer,
chewing on limes, occasionally smoking
some wonderful dope.
Odilón started speaking Nahuatl, but
Number 3 only grinned at the indigenous chatter.
He lit up a Delicado and waved his hand at me.
I was sure he had horns on his monstrous head.
He wanted more tequila.
I took a long slug, then passed him the bottle.
Saint Francis of Assisi, the same for whom
the hotel was named, the same
who never gives up talking to the birds,
the innocent animals,
this same Saint dangled from the cracked rearview mirror.
I prayed to Saint Francis that he find me safe passage.

Time passed like it always does.

¿A donde vamos? I asked Odilón after a while,
wanting both of these Mexicans to know
that I could understand their Spanish.

Nowhere, he said and patted
his coifed grey hair into place,
he straightened his black bowtie.

He told me not to worry, told me
not to speak any more Spanish.
I was getting paid good money, wasn't I?

Fuck you, I said.

Odilón only smiled at my anger.
He asked me if I was a poet.

Shit no, I said.

That's good, he said.

Time passed some more.

We sped thru the rainy night,
ascending first into the foothills, then
into black winding canyon roads
all the time climbing toward timberline.
But taxis will only go so far into the ambiguity,
so Number 3 slammed on the brakes
and fish-tailed to a stop.
I couldn't see anything.

                              Odilón
said in a drunken English
that it was the end of the line for me,
that it had been a pleasure.
He added that I didn't owe anybody jackshit.

                              Okay, I said,
got out and waved goodbye,
but the taxi rojo had already spun around
and left me in the gringo gloom .

Mexicans think that all white people are stupid,
but that's not true.
I've been around longer than most folks,
I know a few things,
picked up wisdom here and there.
Like in the Blood of Christ Mountains
where the Jew named Max and a girl from Beaver College
fixed me up with a bag of tricks.
I never go anywhere without my bag of tricks.
Inside was a little magic prayer
that said I wanted
the trees and the stars
to welcome me like family,
and, by God, they did just that.
They gave me beans and tortillas, they
scolded me for drinking the tequila,
they introduced me to a young woman
with hair like the blue side of the moon.
My name is Sofía, she said,
and she took me into a warm cave,
she bathed me,
she sang lullabies that told stories
about heroes and gods walking the green earth,
she lay down beside me
(her body like a river after summer rain)
until I found the lonely path into my dreams.
She was not in those dreams,
nor was she there the next morning
when I woke up, shivering and cold.
She was nowhere to be found.
The mountains were only mountains again.

The sun had run its miraculous course
thru the underside of the earth, returning
glorious as promised
in the lullabies that Sofía had sung.
In the distance Toluca sat like a blister
in a cup of the polluted highlands.
There was nothing to be done.
I started walking and hitchhiking back to the Hotel San Francisco.
It wasn't 15 minutes before a truck stopped.
It's rickety bed was piled high with watermelons
that an old Indian man was taking to the market in Toluca.
His mujer was riding shotgun,
a little Indian boy was sitting between them
with black eyes
that were dark pits leading straight to his roots.
The old man didn't say anything,
just pointed to the back of the truck.
I climbed into a nest of melons and straw
and the truck rattled off toward Toluca.
I was happy to be alive.
I nestled up among the watermelons,
ready for sleep,
when something caught my eye,
a glint in the sunlight
from the corner of the truck.
I poked around some and found a gun barrel.
Then another.
And another.
AK-47s.
Uzis.
Maybe 50 guns altogether.

Holy shit, I thought and looked up
to see the little black-eyed boy laughing at me
through the back window of the truckcab.
I reached inside my shirt
to make sure
I still had my bag of tricks.
Thank God it was there.
I breathed easier
and broke open one of the watermelons
to quench my thirst with the delicious red flesh.
The sun felt good on my body.
I slept.

I woke up in the twilight of some afternoon.
The old man never said a word to me, just
slammed on his brakes
at the front door of the Hotel San Francisco.
I had never told him where I was staying,
but I was too tired to worry about forebodings.
I climbed out of my nest.
The glass door swiveled open.
Beethoven's 9th was playing live from Salt Lake City.
Hallelujah. Hallelujah.
The desk clerk picked at his nose.
He smiled, he said that
Room 717 had been ransacked.
My clothes, my money, my snubnose .38,
all of my things were gone.
A message scribbled on the bathroom mirror with black lipstick
said I had passed the first test and I was now a member of
some long-winded revolutionary force.

The message said to stay put and await further orders.
I needed some coffee, I needed to think.
Lucky for me the restaurant was open.
The new waiter was this guy, Moisés,
the same one with the beard. He
whispered in my ear
that his real name was Rafa Guillén.
He told me not to worry.
Sit down and have a comida,
a cup of café con leche too, he said.
I could stay as long as I liked.
My bills had been paid forever.

## The phone rings
## in the 6 a.m. darkness

The phone rings in the 6 a.m. darkness,
and it's my mother
80 years old
twice widowed
who of course wants to come
to El Paso for a visit,
she wants to be here,
she says,
when the newspaper gives me an award
authorizing
that I am a famous poet,
at least here in El Paso.
Which is not much, I tell her.
Don't say that, she says.
So what should I say?
That I'm standing here in my silk boxer shorts
with a 52-year-old hard-on drifting away
like a luminous green hummingbird
while some other man (evil,
he had a blonde mustache, he carried a gun)
who I found last night in my red meaty heart
was still eating at his 39-cent hamburger
and picking at the ragged white bread,
the scummy bit of cheese.
I suddenly feel like I'm 17 years old again.
Did I get drunk last night?
Did I wreck the car?

No, this is thirty-five years later,
and my mother is apologizing for waking me up,
she forgot it's so early here.
I tell her not to worry,
she can call anytime,
come whenever she wants to,
she's earned that right,
lugging me around in her own heart
for all these years.
She decides to come.
Wonderful, I say,
then I tell her Goodbye, I love you.
I climb back into the warm bed
while the light of day makes its noise
with sparrows and finches and grackles,
and the woman who is my wife,
who is the mother of our three children,
opens her eyes and asks me,
What are you thinking about?
I tell her that I am thinking about my mother,
poor lady, she knows she is dying,
she wants to come visit for a while
but really I want to tell my wife,
about the ungodly man
—the one with the gun and the blonde mustache—
who was wandering those streets of who I am,
he wanted to tell me something,
he wanted to show me the house where I was born?

## It's Sunday Morning, and Socrates and His Buddy Plato Drop by for a Visit

SUDDENLY, in my own backyard, the illustrious fuckup Socrates and his buddy Plato gathered themselves up out of the morning mist and started arguing about art and its purpose in society. After a few opening parries on either side, white-haired Socrates—with that autocratic smile of his that really looked more like a grimace—said that he had been contemplating this very issue during those few rhapsodic moments when he feasted on the hemlock. The old man paused, knowing full well that this allusion to his historic performance had Plato over a barrel. Then he took a deep breath and sat down in a white plastic chair that only the day before I had bought at Sam's Club for $8.95. From the way Plato rolled his eyes in dismay, I took this to mean that Socrates was about to speak in length on the question of reality.

He was right.

For the next hour or so, the ancient carried on about the dark spaces found in the human soul, contending that only through the various candles of music, poetry, painting, sculpture, and, yes, even drama and the making of movies, could these gloomy crannies of our psyche be illuminated and thereby understood. It was true, Socrates stated, that what is presented is many times ugly and despicable, even dangerous to the Body Politic. Yet, his point was (he was jabbing his finger into the air when he said this) that what is below in this incoherent vale of tears only reflects what is above in the land of the holy.

His argument went on to assert that only through all aspects of human endeavor—art, religion, philosophy, mathematics, science, politics, war, economics, medicine, engineering, the art of buying and selling, and all other forms of our craziness—can we discover some complete idea of the Real.

All the time Socrates was talking, Plato nervously paced back and forth on the concrete slab in front of my office, walking in and out of the shadows cast by the morning sun. At particular points, he shook his head in violent disagreement with Socrates' rationale, but he was sufficiently respectful of his teacher to keep his mouth shut. Still, I could tell he couldn't wait to get back to his pen and paper so he could argue with the old bastard in the silence of his writing space.

Socrates really didn't care what Plato thought anyway. Nor did I since I had already read most of what the younger Greek considered valid in *The Republic*, and I could guess within a rat's ass how he would counter the Socratic verbosity.

For that matter, I didn't pay much attention to Socrates either, especially after the first 15 minutes or so. I grew bored with his monologue. The old man certainly didn't take into account my sister Peggy who that same morning lay in the white light of an operating room in Houston, Texas. The doctors opened up her uterus only hours before the words of all shapes and sizes were spilling forth from the mouth of the legendary Socrates. The doctors found there, exploding from the side of an ovary, a tumor the size of grapefruit, and in the surrounding flesh flowered a garden of cancerous cells. Such beauty, hooked like it was to the Angel of Death, gives the lie to Socrates, Plato and their relentless cohorts.

Maybe I'm right and maybe I'm wrong. I don't know. But that's what I told those assholes anyway. Then I told them to get the fuck out of my backyard and go home where they belong.

## Poets Have Few Things To Say

Poets have few things to say,
and this is one of them—
you should not
have stolen that money from your mother.
She'll report it to God.
God lives around the corner from us
with a man She's not married to,
a black trucker from Milwaukee.
The night before he takes off on the long haul,
he eats a big T-bone steak,
he sucks down a six-pack of Bud longnecks
and then he likes a good romp in the sack.
That's where God comes in.
The next morning Her old man is off across America
in a purple truck he calls the Holy Ghost.
God has to go back to Her own business.
She opens the mail.
There's a letter from your mother.

# The News from Armageddon
## In Five Parts

### I.

THE REPUBLICAN GUARD caught Saddam Hussein beating off in the Presidential Bunker while the B-52s bombarded Baghdad. Ignoring protocol, they grabbed his dick and chopped it off at the root. George Bush received the information third-hand and passed it along to Gorbachev. Gorby, he said, you'll never guess. Then he told him. At first they thought it was a good joke. Ha. Ha. But then, after consulting with aides conversant with Arab culture, they didn't know whether to be happy or sad. Neither understood, of course, the ramifications of such an act. How could they?

But Yitchak Shamir did.

The President of Israel called all of his soon-to-be-deployed forces back home and immediately began to sue for peace. Meanwhile, here in America, Billy Graham went on national television (all stations carried the broadcast live, except for CBS and its affiliates) to make sure that we all understand about the End of the World.

"It is near," Billy said, "our time has come, and we must be ready."

## 2.

THE CANOE, which carries two men, floats along on a flat mirror-like lake. The men are looking for birds, preferably fat greasy ducks, to kill and to carry home for food. A large cat (from the looks of her, a normal everyday gray and black house cat) creeps along on top of the mirror. She likes the coolness on her belly. Her eyes glisten like gold. She is Jesus Christ Reincarnate. She wants to talk, to make a deal.

"Hey," she says, "I'll trade my golden eyes for both paddles."

A good deal on most any other day, but land is nowhere in sight and the men don't have any food. Their families are starving. Water, of course, is plentiful although it tastes bitter and smells of urine. The cat really doesn't care about the men's problems. She wants the paddles and she gives them no choice. She hands over her eyes, laying them down inside the canoe. The cat's eyes are so heavy that the canoe sits two inches deeper in the water. Any sort of waves and the canoe will be swamped. The two men become terribly afraid. They look at the cat, they see her empty eye sockets where termites are gnawing at her brain, and they ask for more time. Just a little more time.

## 3.

THE LITTLE GIRL (three years old), who had just witnessed the birth of her baby sister, said that the baby did not come out of her mother's mouth, which is what she expected, but the baby came from "down there." She pointed her little finger to where she meant. She shrugged her shoulders. It didn't make sense to her, but if that is what happens, then that is what happens.

## 4.

AFTER THE MOTHER OF ALL BATTLES began, Maureen pulled on her black body stocking over her fresh nakedness. The cotton panel at the crotch had an opening. She smiled and sipped at her burgundy, and Sammy, after smelling of her body, decided that Bingo could wait for another week. He flicked on his telephone answering machine. Incoming calls could wait too. But he did finish watching a U.S. Marine battery sergeant from World War II who was being interviewed on CNN. The man knew exactly what the soldiers in Kuwait and Iraq were going through. Hadn't he been at Iwo Jima? Hadn't he seen his best friend die from enemy gunfire, a direct hit right behind the ear?

That time it was the Japs and the Nazis.

Then it was the Koreans.

Then the Viet Cong.

But these things must be done, the old man said, that is the nature of man.

Sammy agreed with the old man, but still he was scared. The screen switched to a map on which the Tigris and Euphrates Rivers were flowing toward the Persian Gulf. That is the Cradle of Civilization, Maureen said, I remember it from school. Sammy took a deep breath and turned the television off.

Maureen giggled—Come on to bed, Sammy, it's a good place to hide.

# 5.

EIGHTY-FIVE to one-hundred thousand persons died their very personal deaths during the allied bombing of Iraq and Kuwait. President Bush did not comment on these figures, and this information, as supplied by the Pentagon, made the second page of the *El Paso Times.*

# Galveston, Texas, #4

There's a green lizard in my motel room
Number 155
in Galveston, Texas,
that looks out onto the Gulf of Mexico.
The room, not the lizard.
The lizard hides behind the curtain.
That's okay with me.
I'm drunk.
That's how come I named the lizard Johnny
after my son
who's in the hospital
because today
he was under the knife,
had a skin graft on his neck.
That's a long story,
too long to tell.
Read some of my other poems
if you really want to know.
Most people don't.
I don't blame them either.
Who wants to know about a burned boy?
Look at me.
I should be praying to all that is holy
for my son whom I dearly love.
Some of the day I did just that.
But now it's all over,
and I find it best to hide myself

in a bottle of red wine
and talk to a green lizard named Johnny.
The lizard told me earlier
that it's okay
to do anything I want to.
We were looking outside at the time,
and there it was,
the wide but randomly vicious breast
of the sacred mother sea.

# The Art of the American Southwest

THE HOLOGRAM was encased inside a six-foot long but slender glass box, and it was the perfect image of a huge popsicle stick that rotates slowly, round and round, so that Paco could witness the damp, freshly chewed and sucked wood. It seemed to him that the stick had only recently been the envoy of sweet cherry ice. He could also make out gargantuan toothmarks and finger-sized splinters that bore testimony to the popsicle stick's exact reality. The anonymous artist had titled the piece "Snow White and the Politics of Violent Revolution" and had installed it into the grimey blue-tiled wall of the Men's Restroom at the downtown Greyhound Bus Station, El Paso, Texas. Paco was one of the few witnesses who figured out the true significance of the piece.

That afternoon he wandered into the lonely Potrillo Mountains that rise up out of the desert to the west of El Paso. In his backpack he carried two quarts of water, a knife, a sleeping bag, and an extra pair of tennis shoes. He carried with him no food or extra clothing, but he left behind his pistol, a Ruger .357 magnum, so that his brother could find it and know that he was alive.

The first night in that empty wilderness, hungry and afraid, he slept at the mouth of a dark cave and dreamed of his dead mother. She was naked, she was smiling, she was dancing very slowly. Paco watched her, glad to be with his mother again. She told him that our lives aren't just pieces of trash that float haphazard down a nameless river. Then she disappeared behind a bush, and Paco heard her laughing. Paco, Paco, she yelled, and he too ducked behind the bush. Look, son, look quickly, his mother said, and she pointed to her crotch where rattlesnakes gooey with afterbirth were dripping from between her legs.

The next morning Paco killed two lizards for food, and he followed the cooing of doves until he found a source of water seeping from a niche in the side of a bony mountain.

Nobody from El Paso ever saw Paco again, although wetbacks crossing in the lonely desert still bring rumors of a hermit who wanders the Potrillo Mountains like a moon that wants to be named and loved.

# *Mother Comes for a Visit*

SUDDENLY Lassie the Dog Hero—sleek golden and white collie, female animal savior—pulls my poor old mother out of the burning forest, pulls her by Mom's 80-year-old wise silvery hair, just this one last time, please.

Mom is glad.

She struggles up out of her bed in the 3 a.m. darkness and wobbles to the bathroom.

She takes a long piss, shoving God and death up under the rug for a while.

She's proud of herself, she says, and she's proud of me because my picture was in the newspaper yesterday.

And she loves me too.

She wants to be sure that I know this before she goes back into the secrecy of her sleep where all of our names are like water constantly rushing downstream.

Mom smiles.

She's delighted that God is not a linguistic phenomenon.

But Lassie the Dog Hero is not done with her work.

She's scratching at the bathroom door, she's barking, she's running back and forth in huge circles. Lassie wants my mother to follow.

# November 18, 1992

*⌢ Letter to Eileen Myles*
*after she lost the 1992 Presidential Election*

Dear Eileen,

You would have made a good
President of the United States
for the few days before
Colin Powell put a bullet
through your Kennedy-like head.
It would be made-for-tv ugly.
It would happen the day you opened
the White House to the Homeless and Hungry.
You would wander down to the Vietnam Memorial,
you would begin reading poems about the names of the dead.
General Powell would walk up to shake your hand.
You would reach out to him, glad
that he's finally changed his mind,
that it's all right
to have a lesbian poet in the White House.
You're glad he's black.
You're a sucker for black generals.
You say: "Hello, Colin."
He nods.
You notice that his eyes look like black berries.
You want to give him a kiss, you want
to lick those beautiful eyes.
You smile, enjoying the contradictions of who you are.
The General pulls a Ruger from his coat, a .357 magnum.

He aims at your head.
The gun frightens you, but
you start to read one last poem anyway.
The poem is about a gay soldier who died in Da Nang.
He was shot by his own captain.
You want to be brave, you want to be heroic,
like the soldier in Da Nang
who spit in the captain's face,
yet still you wonder
where the Secret Service is.
I'm sorry, Eileen, but they are hiding in the Rose Garden.
They want you dead too because
you are the first true-to-life lesbian they ever met,
and they are afraid for their daughters,
they are afraid for their wives,
they are afraid for their own selves.
They've heard stories.

The General pulls the trigger.
Clickety-clack.
Horseman, pass by.

Dan Rather is delighted.
And can you imagine George Will?
It would be the best thing since
Jack Ruby and Lee Harvey Oswald
did their little dance for us.
Assassination would become kosher.
It won't be murder, it won't be homicide,
it will be "the necessity of the state."

Think about yourself lying
in the grass at the Vietnam Memorial,
your life dripping away
into the manicured lawn while
the General sneaks into the night
with his entourage of well-wishers
like a scene out of *Julius Caesar*.
Some of the weary Veterans are cursing you,
others are dragging you away,
a fallen hero to their righteous cause.
But none of them really care about you,
who you really were, a poet
doing theater among the holy of holies,
then, strangely caught
in a web of histories none of us
expected or really understood

—*LESBIAN WINS PRESIDENCY*—

no, they just want work,
they want three square meals a day,
life and liberty,
the pursuit of happiness,
some sex every now and then
to cut into their sorrow,
that's all they want
—that's maybe all we really want, huh?


Your followers are terrified.
They break rank.
They are afraid.
The National Guard, secretly

mobilized the week before,
begins to break into
radio and TV stations across the country.
Your vice-president
                    —Alice Notley?
                    Wanda Coleman?—
is under house arrest.

The important thing, though,
is none of this ever happened.
You are alive and well.
So is Bill Clinton, you might say.
Ditto George Bush.
Even Ross Perot.
They got bucks for the dentist,
they don't have to worry about doctor bills,
they don't have to go to the grocery store.
You're right, of course.
I don't disagree.
But you're writing poems.
None of those fools are writing poems.
They couldn't if they wanted to.
That is your glory.

*Big deal, right?*

I know that's what we all thought
when we were 25.
But still, being a poet,
fiddling around with the language
that people got to speak
and use

means something.
It has to.
At least to me
because,
shit, Eileen,
I still write poems.
That's what I enjoy
doing.
It's truly the real work that I have.

I should say here that I voted for you
but I won't because I didn't.
For once I wanted to vote for a winner.
Forgive me. I was wrong.

                    Love,
                        Bobby

# City Life

The worm was brown, maybe three feet long,
thick and furry like a caterpillar,
sexless, it
wrapped itself around
the woman's arm and began to gnaw at her flesh.
Luckily I was on the street to help her.
I lit a Camel filter cigarette
and burned out the worm's eyes.
It squirmed some, then fell
onto the pavement and dissolved
into goo like a salted snail.
The woman, a brunette
who let herself be warmed
with blue cashmere,
was delighted.
She introduced herself as Alice,
she called me Sweets,
she kissed me in the ear,
but she said she didn't have the time
to repay my bravery
with the favors of her love

because

(here she paused and whispered secretly)

she was on her way to Mexico
to buy holy artifacts

blessed by the tongues of shamans.
That was okay with me.
I had to get to the K-Mart before it closed
to pick up some underwear and a bottle of cheap vitamin-C.

# Timothy's Struggles with God

When he was only 13 years of age
Timothy repented of his lust, thus found
in one of those sacred ironies of the Real
the secrets of his sex
beneath a bedspread of assorted animal pelts
in Mary Magdalene's room.
But it wasn't enough to absolve him of all sin,
so he prayed earnestly to God
to please loosen
the strings of his angry soul.
He didn't want to give up, he prayed,
like his blasphemous father
the suicide
who died beating his bloody fists
against the ubiquitous Holy Ghost.
God, of course, would never relent.
That's not the point, an angel whispered
sweetly in Timothy's ear.
Ten years later, the twine
of his soul still tightly knotted,
Timothy got a job bartending at the King's X.
He wasn't good at his work
so he got all the lousy shifts.
That was okay by him—
he didn't need much money,
he didn't need the whisky either.
No, what he needed was to find some way

to lose himself forever
as hero
in the perfect struggle against the adversary
who he was still unable to name.
So in the quiet dark hours
on Tuesday or Wednesday nights,
when the drunks shuffled around
the streets of the city
like last Sunday's newspaper,
Timothy taught himself to flip
maraschino cherries with a spatula.
He discovered real power in this art,
and he got so good he could shoot down
heavenly angels
floating in the black night sky.
One unclean night, still
plumbing the depth of his father's anger,
Timothy strode outside the King's X
and saddled one of the stray
melancholy horses of the Apocalypse.
Poor Timothy.
He was last seen terrorizing,
nay, violating,
the trunks of live oak trees
which—he swore
to any man, woman or child
foolish enough to listen—
were the intimate mansions of God.

## Unintelligible Drunken Memo to Myself Written on an Unlined 3x5 Index Card

I can't buy understanding for $3.50 a shot anymore,
not since Carl Jung and all his buddies took a hike,
leaving the Sportsman Lounge tangled up
with Sunday afternoon football games and economic theory,
exquisite peroxided-blonde villainous females
dressed in black panties and delicate bras
shooting dumdum bullets of reality at my mother,
poor old lady, widowed by the disaster of war
and charged with the need to be a bread-winning householder,
thereby made whole and holy through the exactitude of random chance,
and all she really wanted to do was spend the whole of her life
bringing me and my dead sister big tumblers full of chocolate milk.

# Tuesday Night, #17

I'm ready to go play basketball
Push my 54–year–old body up and down the court
Maybe get drunk later
at the L&J Bar and Restaurant
Eat an order of taquitos
Yell at Felipe Hernández about
his goddamn rightwing politics
But the phone is ringing
It's el Subcomandante Marcos
in the jungle of Mexican sorrow
He wants to send his passion
across the planet
via an AT&T satellite
I whisper a distracted Hello
and I hear indigenous guns clicking
in the static of the English language
I ask him: Are you all right
Can I call you back later
El Sup laughs a gentle laugh
He doesn't want me to be late
to el basket, mis cuates
running up and down the court
en tenis y shorts
He says Good luck, he says
all he wants is to sleep alone
and at peace under a tree
in the mountains of Chiapas

The phone clicks dead

I hope they don't kill him
I hope that he doesn't die

~ *September 1994*

# How to Eat Stuffed Fish in Juárez

Jesus died for the sins of us all.
So I walked across the bridge to Mexico
with my friend Rus the basketball coach,
and we ate fish at the Villa del Mar
which seemed like
the natural thing to do—
it was Lent in a Catholic country.
The waiter was a pro, thank God.
Two Bohemias apiece,
chips and fresh pico de gallo,
bolillos (on the soft side)
a good and simple caldo,
the pescado was rellenado
con tiny shrimp and crabmeat.
The bill was 16 bucks and we added a four dollar tip,
becoming heroes because we had money in our pockets.

Outside the afternoon had become night.
The glass doors opened,
and like always
there was the river
of dark fleshy people
who walked up and down
like they knew where they were going.
Hallowed be their names.
Hallowed be all of our names.
We went and said Hello to Benito Juárez,
stern el presidente indígena

gloriously astride a marble and bronze pedestal
in the exact center of a plaza
that carried his name like secret ammunition.
Pancho Villa and Emilio Zapata
were somewhere in the shadows of the flimsy trees,
happy to be the guardians of a pair of lovers
who were snuggled up on a green park bench.
The man had his hand inside the woman's white blouse.
We turned back into the clutter of human beings,
the clanging traffic,
and a little Tarahumara brother and sister who found us
like lost pieces of a puzzle, blessed us
with their sad hunger, their black watery eyes
blinking with the memory of

> the Sierra Madre,
> hunger,
> narcotraficantes,
> dead babies,
> lost Gods.

All that we had to give was money.
50¢ for each of them.
Enough so that they fled back to their mother,
a tiny woman who sat on the curb with another baby
wrapped in a rebozo that was becoming the color of night.

It would have been nice
to have had my wife along beside me,
friend and lover, a woman
to touch my hand crossing the confused streets.

But Rus was okay—

he listened to the disturbances in my sentences
like a friend is supposed to do,
at least until he ran into a British travel-writer-novelist-acquaintance
who towed along a wife and a blonde couple from Baltimore,
all of them younger than me, all of them
delighted with who they were and who
they were going to be.
I should have told them about my brother Bill,
59-years-old,
whose heart burst open one morning
two months before
after he had bagged his limit one last time
of beautiful mallard ducks
from the cold Mississippi sky.
The Holy Trinity—

God the Holy Blood,
God the Holy Dead,
God the Holy Food.

I didn't because
this was Mexico and Mississippi is Mississippi
and my brother was dead now
forever.
So there we all were
five gabachos on the other side
with nothing to talk about
except ourselves.
We avoided the subject for the most part.
At least we didn't talk about basketball.
Thank you, Jesus.
I bought a bottle of Tequila and went home.

## like the creek

running muddy
which is what Lao-tzu
said, me full of

wine,
the nightness
filled

with simply night
and fireflies blinking
sentimental

hellos and blessings,
may
my brother's soul

wander safely among
the dark and gooey
grasses, snakes

and bugs
eyeing his passage
into another world.

*∼ Dobie Ranch, Early Spring, 1997*

## The United States of America

Adolfo Rodríguez is a Mexican.
He never really wanted to come to
the United States of America.
He never wanted his children
speaking a language he didn't
understand, would
never understand. He
didn't want the alcoholism
that came with his friends, his
brother, the long hours after
work on the roofing crews,
drinking the night away. He
didn't want the strange men
babbling furious Spanish and
tearing at him with their fists,
their knives. He didn't want
to witness his own bloody
drunken sorrow curled into a broken body.
He didn't want his son seeing him like that,
measuring him against other men,
cursing him for his weakness. He
never wanted the diabetes
eating at his flesh and soul
like a hoard of ants, slowly,
until he was only a shell
of the handsome man who married his
beloved wife. He didn't want
his beautiful black eyes to drip

with the bitter tears
into the thick grass of his
gringo neighbor's yard. He never
never wanted to come here.
He came anyway. Lo hice para el dinero,
he said. The money. Siempre el dinero.
And for his wife and kids.
They were the ones who wanted to come.

# July in the Desert of Chihuahua

You got to learn to live
in the Chihuahua Desert.
It can be hard.
Especially in the summer
before the pitiful rains of August
come along and wash away all understanding.
Like in July when it becomes so hot
that every year
God has to send along special emissaries
to El Paso
to teach the faithful
the true meaning of heat.
It can be a difficult lesson to learn.
This year it happened so quick—
those two days
during the whole hot summer
when we got to feast on
a harvest of real juicy tomatoes.
Everyone was stuffing themselves with tomatoes,
and the sidewalks were sticky
with the thick juices of those tomatoes.
The tomatoes were the gift of a fat Mexican named José.
He was an illegal immigrant
who looked like he belonged on Channel 44
talking to beautiful blonde showgirls
with enormous breasts.
Instead, he came along and started
passing out the Big Boys

that he smuggled across the Rio Grande.
Meanwhile his wife Maria was doing
a fancy little two-step
to the hard screeching glare
of Mariachi trumpets.
On the second day José had no more tomatoes.
He was done.
He smiled at the gathered throng,
unzipped his jeans and peed lustily
into the dusty hot gutter.
"We are proud and happy,"
he said in Spanish, "to have saved you all."
José and Maria then disappeared into
the downtown Jack-in-the-Box
where they bought two large chocolate milkshakes,
two Big Jacks and two regular orders of fries.
The order was "para llevar."
The exact second they walked back out into the streets
two homeless men
(one a black man, the other a gringo)
died from dehydration
and went straight to Heaven
where they were given clothes, food
and a place at the front of the line.
Rumor has it that
Jesus was watching from Room 333 of the Plaza Hotel.
He, of course, understood everything already,
and, thus secure in his enlightenment,
jumped back into the sack with Maria de Magadelena.
¿Me amas? he asked.
Yo te amo, she said.

The rest of us simply contemplated the meaning of these messages.
We crossed ourselves, we said a prayer,
then we stood in the heat
talking quietly about what had happened.
When finally the darkness came
with its little bit of cool breeze
we went about business as usual,
not quite sure yet if we understood
this newest homily from God.

# Whatever Happened to Art in America?

ONE WEDNESDAY MORNING in the winter of 1993 Art in
America woke up as usual at 5:30, stretched his arms and
then tried to forget the dream about the dark warm room at
the top of a desert hill on the other side of the Rio Grande
100 yards inside the mysterious apparatus we call Mexico.

His father had climbed that hill too, Art had been talking to him,
finally, after all these years. The two men—Art in America
was at last man enough to look steadily into his father's
black eyes—talked about the chance of a Super Bowl game
between the Dallas Cowboys and the mean blitzing Hous-
ton Oilers.

Art in America hated Buddy Ryan, so did his father, they were
glad of that, but Junior wondered out loud why his mother
never walked into his dreams anymore, never fixed him a
meal again, her menudo so thick with pozole but only a
little bit of tripe.

His father didn't know and really didn't care. Arturito always wanted
too much, he said. He wished that he had never crossed
the river, he should never have taken Art and his sister
Cecilia a los States.

Art in America heard the electric alarm ringing and so he quickly
put his father aside, he had to get ready for work. Work is

the important thing, he told himself every morning of his life, so he got up out of bed, mumbled his morning prayers that always asked La Señora de Guadalupe to watch after his sister and himself, both alone now in the United States of America. He hated himself for saying these prayers, it was unmanly, but he could never make himself stop.

Art walked to the bathroom in his bedraggled slippers, turned on the shower, stripped and stepped inside, remembering his mother again because he saw her there in the darkness, smiling to say hello, just as he was falling, disappearing into that small bright hole that miraculously appeared in the scummy blue linoleum of the bathroom floor.

After lunch a woman from work called Art in America's sister Cecilia.

No, she didn't know where Art was, and, yes, his absence was strange. Everybody knew that Art hated to miss work. His desk at work and the Dallas Cowboys—these were the two principle concepts that pasted Art in America's life together.

Cecilia was worried, so she arranged to meet the three women from his work at his house.

They rang the doorbell, they knocked hard on the back door, they rattled the windows, but nothing. Finally, they called the police who came and broke through the back door. Mr. Martinez, they yelled, but nobody answered. They looked into each room until they found Art in America stretched out on the cold bathroom floor. He was still alive, he had been there for seven hours.

Three weeks later Art in America was lying on clean white sheets in a hospital bed, his eyes wide open. He stared up out of that little innermost hole that he found in his bathroom floor. Sometimes he felt his mother trying to push him back up through that hole, other times she was pulling at him. He wanted to tell somebody that his mother was trying to help, but he couldn't talk, he couldn't move his body. All he could do was sometimes squeeze a finger when somebody was asking him questions.

Art, this is Billy, your neighbor. Remember me? Do you know who I am?

Art in America squeezed my finger. His sister said he was angry. He's always been angry. That's his secret, she said. And now he wants to go to work. But that will never be. Never again.

The End.

# The Price of Groceries

I buy my groceries in a place called Quality Foods.
It's only five miles from the U.S./Mexico Border.
They sell Schlitz beer.
Schlitz smells like when I growing up in Memphis.
It's $3.99 a 12-pack.
I drink a lot of Schlitz.
Quality has some good bananas,
lots of golden delicious apples,
the meat's okay,
especially the brisket.
And the checkout girl knows who I am.
Her name is Monette.
She always says Hello, she cashes my checks.
She is pretty the way America used to be pretty
back in the 50s after the War
when I was wanting to be a man.
Remember Doris Day? Remember Rock Hudson?
Monette's breasts aren't too large,
they're just about perfect.
Every day she wears orange socks.
She looks me in the eye—like Doris,
Monette has blue eyes, she has blonde hair,
she has a freckled face—
she says she is God's gift from the State of Missouri,
but she won't go back there no more.
Too much rain, too many floods.
She says she likes Mexicans, she likes the way they talk,

so she's learning a few words of Spanish.
Mucho gusto, she says.
She says she sees the writing on the wall.
She sells me a pack of Camel cigarettes.
I buy a newspaper too.
The Serbs are killing the Bosnians,
the Bosnians are killing the Serbs.
Monette smiles.
On Wednesday nights, she says,
she dances naked at the Paradise Cafe.

# Breaking and Entering

## I.

LAST NIGHT, after everybody in the neighborhood had gone to sleep, I slipped down to Dickie Escobar's house and shot him in the side of the head with a poem.

It was easy.

No moon in the sky, the street like a rotten slice of meat.

A pit bull struggled against his chain and barked uselessly at my shadow.

I navigated through assorted beer cans, two empty pint bottles of Popov Vodka, a dirty Pampers, the smell of piss.

The door was open.

I knew that his old mother Espie and his half-wit sister Isabel slept in the back room, their arms wrapped around each other. Isabel is worried that her mother is shrinking away to nothing. Each morning a little bit of flesh and bone has been stolen by God.

## 2.

ISABEL hates God.

God's not fair.

Isabel clutches at her mother. She smiles at everybody she sees. She carries that smile from place to place like it's a suitcase. Only a few people know what is inside.

Isabel is afraid that her mother will float away to Heaven like her father did. She doesn't want to be left alone with Dickie. She's afraid of his friends. They get drunk, they use bad words, they fight, the police come with their guns, the flashing lights. Sometimes they take Dickie away. Espie cries. The old woman curses the police. She won't sleep.

Isabel holds her mother's hand and smiles.

Isabel watches while God goes to work stealing the flesh and bone of her mother.

## 3.

ISABEL wishes that God would put Dickie in the fancy box and take him away to Heaven to live with the angels.

She makes this prayer to God.

God doesn't do what Isabel wants.

This is why Isabel hates God.

# 4.

I WALKED into the living room like I belonged there, like I was plumber ready to fix a leak, like I was a French hero in a novel with a job to save the Free World.

The living room smelled of stale beer and cigarette smoke. The television was left on, but nothing was there, only a dark blue blinking haze to give me sufficient light to go about my business.

Dickie was asleep on the couch in his dirty underwear. He looked handsome in the little bit of light, his long brown body squirming in dreams I wanted to conjure with my poem. A tattoo engraved into the muscle of his right arm advertised Black Sabbath, another on his left arm waved the flag of mota. The sign over his heart said, I Love My Mom.

I moved toward him quietly.

A quart bottle of Budweiser beer slipped out of his slender hand and rattled around on the floor.

Dickie opened his black eyes.

I said: Dickie, I have something for you.

What? he asked.

I pulled the trigger.

It was my last resort.

# 5.

DICKIE WATCHED the blue hummingbird with the long curved beak make love to the white blossom. It was a prodigious blossom, big enough to slip a hand into.

It dangled from a banana tree.

Dickie followed the hummingbird to the next tree, then to the next.

The hummingbird led him up a slender trail into the mountainous jungle.

A stream of blue water snaked through the trees and vines.

The stream went downhill.

# 6.

DICKIE STOPPED FOLLOWING the hummingbird so that he could watch the fishes. They were feeding on black berries and the eggs of insects. They carved little round nests in the sand. One fish laid eggs into the nest, another fish swam into the nest with manly intentions.

Dickie couldn't tell one fish from the other.

He built himself a boat. He wanted to learn about the fishes.

## 7.

DICKIE GOT OUT of the boat and sat down in the surf.

He let the waves gnaw at his slender brown body.

Nobody had said a word to him in three weeks.

He was happy.

He took off his underwear.

The foam and muck of the ocean gathered in his pubic hair.

Dickie splashed the salty green water onto his genitalia.

Seagulls circled in the blue sky.

The seagulls cried for bread to eat, but Dickie didn't know how to bake bread.

His mother did.

Dickie wanted to find his mother. He'd have to go home, but he didn't know how to get home.

He stopped at the Circle-K and bought a map for $2.50. With tax the map cost $2.71. He had enough money left over for a Coca-Cola Classic and a victory cigar. The clerk gave him a free pack of matches.

Here, the clerk said.

Dickie said, Thanks.

## 8.

I SAW DICKIE walking down the street and waved at him. He was carrying a map, he had on a new pair of blue jeans. He wasn't wearing a shirt. He looked handsome and proud, his black eyes like polished stone.

It's a nice day, I said.

Yea, he said, but I hope it rains. The desert needs the rain.

He smoked a cigarette and looked at the blue sky like he knew what he was talking about. Maybe he did. He offered me a cigarette.

Thanks, I said, and we looked at the blue sky together.

Then I said: How's your mom and Isabel?

Oh, they're fine, he said.

I'm glad, I said.

# An Elegy for Joe Brainard

~ *August 17, 1994*

I REMEMBER Joe Brainard never coming to El Paso. Maybe he stopped at the bus station or the airport and looked at the incredibly burnished blue sky—so bright that it hurt his eyes—before he got back on the bus or the airplane and went wherever he was going. But I doubt it. Or maybe he came to Albuquerque when I was there. Or Las Cruces or Alamosa or South Fork or Galveston even, but I doubt that too. The point is I never met Joe Brainard.

I remember that Joe Brainard and I were born in the same year which was 1942. Joe was born in Salem, Arkansas, but his family moved to Tulsa. I was born in Memphis and stayed right there for a long time.

I remember coming home from Mexico City last Monday night at 10:30 PM after being there for two months and having to wait around until after midnight because our two boys who are almost grown men didn't know enough to leave or go to bed and the house wasn't empty enough nor quiet enough so that Lee and I could finally make love. I remember two days later which was this morning only ten minutes ago and picking up the *Poetry Flash* and seeing a photograph of a painting of Joe Brainard by Tom Clark and reading a Tom Clark poem that said Joe Brainard is dead.

Then I remembered Mexico City, me sitting in a bar and drinking an ice cold Negro Modelo and somebody telling me that

Joe Brainard had died of AIDS and it hurt me almost to tears, but I soon forgot about his death and my sadness until right now when I was writing this Joe-Brainard-like poem because when I was in Mexico City I was writing a lot and talking in Spanish, and El Paso where I never met Joe Brainard was a long way away.

I remember driving my white Dodge Ram pickup truck from Florida to Atlanta to see my daughter, then to Memphis to see my mother and finally back home to El Paso, and on that long trip I read Joe Brainard's book *I Remember* outloud to myself at least twice while going 75 miles an hour on Interstate Highways where there is enough slack in reality so that I really didn't have to pay attention. That was in April of 1990 and Joe and I were both about to be 48 years old.

I remember that I tried to write "I remember" poems for months afterwards I read *I Remember* by Joe Brainard but I couldn't because I wasn't innocent enough or I had some equally difficult problem with my heart which obviously Joe Brainard never had. Or maybe he did.

I remember a friend telling me that it's impossible to lie in a poem or a dream. I think she was a little extreme, don't you? I think Joe Brainard would have thought she was a little extreme, too. He would have told her so. Not me. Which is another reason I miss Joe Brainard even though I never met him and I even forgot about him that time in Mexico City after I learned he was dead.

# The Sign on Interstate 10

The sign on Interstate 10 says,
If You Want to Know the Lord,
Call 532-6755.
I've always wanted to know the Lord,
so when I got home I called 532-6755.
A woman answered the phone.
Her English was just about as good
as my Spanish, but we could talk.
She said her name was Maria,
and she said the Lord wasn't in.
She said the Lord was playing in the Finals
of the Sun Carnival Handball Tournament
at the Downtown YMCA.
Which didn't seem fair to me.
I asked if the Lord had a cellular.
She said no, but she could tell me
all that I wanted to know.
What's that? I asked.
Know thyself, she said in her broken English.
That's about the whole package, she said,
although there's some extras.
What kind of extras? I asked.
Oh, she said, things like
How-To manuals and road maps.
The extras cost money.
She said the Lord takes
Visa, Mastercard and American Express.

# *The Rules of Engagement, 1997*

I was on the wrong side of lost.
The door in front of me was a naïve yellow,
the knob was hot, the thick wall white-washed adobe,
and outside an empty dump truck
caked with red river mud was waiting for me.
Danny Natividad, the driver, was the proverbial Mexican—
skinny with the mustache,
the white 10–gallon Stetson and blue jeans,
fancy lizard skin boots and a pearl-buttoned cowboy shirt.
Outlaw money was no mystery to him.
Danny looked at me with dark blistered eyes.

I asked him, "Where the hell am I?"

"Redford," he said, "Redford, Texas,
across the Rio Grande from México,
population 107,
a place so uninhabited of gabachos
that words in English are dead seeds planted in the dust."

Danny's English was perfect though, so perfect
that I was afraid of what he wanted with me.
He flicked the butt of a Lucky Strike cigarette at the desert's horizon.

He said, "I am your guide into the beast.
You will get paid when you tell this story
to somebody who understands. You gabachos
cannot hear our corridos, the bajo sexto
does not strum that sad music into your hearts."

The huge sky was metallic blue, the sun
like a ball-peen hammer tapping at the inside of my skull.
"Okay, okay," I said, and I made the long climb
into the cab of the truck where waiting for me
was our ubiquitous brown mother screwed into the dashboard.
On the cracked seatcover two six-packs of Budweiser longnecks
were icing in a plastic bag,
and a calendar hanging from a knob
pictured a naked woman caressing a very large wrench.
The woman was blonde and blue-eyed,
red lips of polished stone,
and she rose up out of a perfect green sea.
The calendar said that the day was 20 de mayo.

Danny Natividad turned the key and the truck rumbled alive,
lurching through the shabby little town of Redford.
An old man who was sitting in front of an abarrotes
picked at his nose and didn't turn his head
when the truck groaned past him, Danny
slipping through the gears with angel grease.
A scrawny line of barren mountains
50 miles away
struggled across the horizon.
We didn't need to go far.
The truck fishtailed into a dirt road
and lumbered downhill toward the Rio Grande.
We stopped
and Danny pointed off into the distance below
where the shallow muddy river twisted like blood
through the tattered landscape,

doing it's job of separating one country from the other.
A herd of maybe forty goats foraged in the chaparral.
A young man waited patiently for the goats.
On the other side of the river another man leaned
against the hood of his pickup
watching the United States of America.

Danny Natividad said:
                    "The boy with the goats,
the shepherd, that's Zeke Junior,
el hijo de Esequiel Hernández.
He has 18 years now, he has the innocent
eyes and ears, like desert flowers
buzzing with hummingbirds and bees.
That old gun he's carrying—
it was his grandfather's 22,
a gun so old and weak it couldn't kill ni un gato.
Not even a sick cat."
Danny popped open two beers and handed me one.
It was ice-cold. Danny took a long slug.
He looked at me out of the corner of his dark eye.

                    He said,

"Mister, I don't know who sent you here to this piece of dirt,
but me, I'm sort of a brujo, a witch,
¿comprendes?
and my job is to show you something you'll never forget,
a story that will rot in your dreams, a story
that keeps telling itself over and over again.
Forever.
Drink as much beer as you want, todo lo que quieres,

but keep your eyeballs on the windshield.
Things will be happening at the edge of who you are.
Do you understand?"

No, I didn't understand, but what could I do?
I sat back in the hot seat and let Danny Natividad tell me
what was happening in the desert
through the pocked glass of his windshield.

He said: "The man on the Mexican side of the river,
his name is Gerónimo Oropeza. He means
absolutely nothing to this story
except he will be la chispa, you know,
the spark that lights the fire.
There is a squad of U.S. Marines in the chaparral.
They are looking at Oropeza, they are
wondering what a man is doing standing there, viendo pa'ca,
looking at America, they are sure
he is a narcotraficante, or maybe a coyote
who will smuggle mojados across the river
to bruise the fabric of who
we Americans are supposed to be.
This is what the Marines have been taught to believe.
And so they are scampering up from the river,
they want to report that Gerónimo Oropeza
is standing on the other side of the Rio Grande
and that he is doing nothing but watching
the United States of America,
and, therefore, he is suspect."

Natividad sighed

and made the sign of the cross on his skinny chest,
the Mother-of-Pearl buttons sparkling in the heat,
then he took a swig of cold beer and continued:
"Look over there, ves,
in the greasewood and the mesquite.
Something's moving in there.
I told you.
It's los pinches Marines.
They see Zeke and his goats, they see
that he's carrying a gun, they think
he's a compañero of Gerónimo Oropeza
because Zeke watered his goats in the river
across from where Gerónimo was watching.

¿Entiendes, Mister? Do you understand?

The Marines have already convicted Zeke
and now they're going to kill him, they're going
to make him a martyr
to their own empty imagination."

*Colonel Kelly told the press: "In order to get the attention of
the individual, Unit 513 would've had to expose themselves.
And there was no requirement under the rules of engagement
about having to do that."*

"Mother of Jesus," I said, wishing
I was watching this story on the 5 o'clock news.
But I wasn't.
I drank more beer.
Sweat dripped from my armpits,
my eyes ached in the sunlight,

there was a disturbance in the bushes,
and I saw an animal rise up against the blue sky.
Then another one, and another one,
like bears walking on their hind legs,
then they disappeared into the scrub.
Ghosts.

"What the fuck?" I said.

Danny Natividad smiled at my nervousness.
He wiped the sweat off his forehead.
Then he started again—

"No te parecen hombres, ¿verdad?
But they are real.
Real as the M-16s that they hug to their chests.

                          Clemente Bañuelos, Jr.,

Ronald Wieler, Jr.,

                          Ray Torres, Jr.

          James Matthew Blood

whose names you should spread
                              like signposts
          across this landscape
                    in your poem

               of a language gone dead

boys

all of them between the ages of 19 and 22
bivouacked here
secretly
camouflaged in the so-called *ghilli* suits
stringy brown and green burlap
duct-tape
faces smeared with oil
sweltering heat
eating rations out of cans
close enough to learn the everyday habits
of the citizens of Redford
and El Polvo
the dumpy town across the river with the name
like the end of the earth

those young men are trained for war
shoot-to-kill
they have lived five days in the dusty loneliness of the desert
greasewood and mesquite
grama grass
rabbits and snakes
little mice
the fauna and flora of religious solitude
these young marines whispering to each other in the darkness
dirty dreams become
masturbation in the silence of cool gray mornings
the turkey vultures circling

hobgoblins

feral beasts

they scampered to higher ground
to find Zeke Junior
bringing his small herd of goats home from water
nervous, gun-ready
a live round chambered into his 22
because
wild dogs had recently ravaged one of the goats."

He was near home now, moving
toward a dilapidated old house where
he had played games as a young boy.
The Marines stalked him, two on each side.
Danny Natividad was drinking his second beer,
I was on my third.
My head ached, the wind blew.

                    Click.
          Click.

Danny said—"What time is it?"
"Six," I said, "give or take 10 minutes."

Danny sat stoned-faced, staring at Zeke
and the goats who were braying
as they wandered back toward their pen.
I wanted to get out of the truck,
I wanted to go tell Zeke to go home,
get the hell away.

                         "Don't even think it,"
Natividad said and spat out the window in disgust.

He said: "Stories must happen.
That is a law of God.
Even the fucking anger, the bleeding sore in my heart,
cannot prevent this story from happening.
Zeke will die his death without even knowing why he was shot.
Those politicians in Washington, they have emptied their souls
and now they wander around
in the cities of America
like they reside at the core of truth.
The desert is like the sun and the moon—
it rides the eternal wheel, but
those men and women walk the flat earth
and they will disappear forever.
That is my curse on those assholes.
Put that in your story when you tell it."

A jackrabbit scurried out of the brush
and stopped in the shade of a greasewood.
Zeke raised his rifle and pulled the trigger.
Bang.
He missed, the rabbit darted away,
he chambered another round,
and silence settled again into the desert,
a silence that refused to go away.

Colonel Kelly said:
*"It is the team's impression that there is no mistake that they were
identified as human."*

Squad leader Clemente Bañuelos
rose up out of the chaparral,

a soldier who was engaged with the enemy,
the M–16 at his shoulder.
He took a deep breath
and squeezed
                    the trigger.
Zeke was turning back to the goats
innocent,
it was time to go home for dinner,
when the shot rang through the wide space,
startling Zeke's father
who was smoking a cigarette
and waiting for his son to come home.
Zeke was already past knowing.
The bullet had entered the soft flesh of his right side
and opened like a black flower,

spinning,
the petals ripping open

the liver
the spleen
the aorta

He staggered, then fell backwards.

Before he died Zeke Junior
heard the goats bleating in the bushes

heard the scruffling of boots
heard a miserable cursing of words

"I capped the mother fucker I put him down."

"O Jesus God"

"O fuck o fuck o fuck"

felt the terrible pain in his chest
his heart emptying of blood
the hot wind of the desert sun blow across his face

and saw

the dark eyes and brown face of Clemente Bañuelos,
a boy like himself, an M–16 in his hands,
the soldier staring down into his bewildered eyes.

Then Zeke Junior crossed over into the wild darkness.
Ding.
Ding.
The four young soldiers
like savage angels
stood and watched
while the soul of
Esequiel Hernández, Jr.
as blood
seeped into the dry ground.

# The Meaning of North Dallas

DANTE, who really does have a screwy Italian accent, showed up in El Paso with his sidekick Virgil and announced to me and my photographer friend Richard that we inhabit either the third or fourth Circle of Hell.

Since I am close to being 52 years old and am therefore concerned how I spend the rest of my life, I was interested in his calculations, but Richard was unperturbed. He, who was born a Jew, pooh-poohed the immortal poet and what he called "that Renaissance wop bullshit." Instead, he concocted up a pitcher of screwdrivers which we all shared like vultures pecking at the scrawny carcass of a jackrabbit.

The booze got the three of them talking about the meaning of existence while I got drunk and angry in my own rather paltry sorrow. After a while I informed them that, goddamnit, I didn't want to live in any Circle of Hell.

Richard laughed at my foolishness and told Dante and Virgil that he didn't give a good rat's ass which Circle of Hell he lived in because on Tuesday he was going to move to North Dallas, buy a condominium and change his name to Rick. He was certain that he'd find a rip in the fabric of truth in that God-forsaken place and then he'd be able to slip out into the darkness before anybody knew he was missing.

# Monday Night Football

At halftime of the game between
the Miami Dolphins and the San Diego Chargers
Frank Gifford, using the miraculous
technology of holographic imagery,
gave Troy Aikman—
who was stretched out on his sofa
in the living room of his home outside Dallas—
a blowjob
in front of millions of fans.
The Cowboy quarterback's turkeyneck
was not quite what we all expected and hoped for.
Still, it was a television first,
and America was somehow satisfied.
The hologram was followed by two commercials,
one showing a Dodge Ram Truck
smashing thru a huge birthday cake
and into the snowy northern woods,
the other depicting a man buried
up to his neck in sand
as he watched a lavishly sexy brunette
in a red string bikini
walk away with his sixpack of Bud Light.
The screen then switched back to Frank
who asked Troy
if he was astonished by the obscenity
of his $50,000,000 contract.
Troy, looking perfectly handsome,
a hero, a man of granite,

but also serene and somehow wise,
thought about the question for a second.
Then he looked directly into the camera,
took a deep breath and said, No.
Frank said Thanks, Troy.
*The Washington Post* reported
in it's Early Morning Edition
that after witnessing the event
President and Hillary Clinton simply
got up off the couch and went to bed.
San Diego, by the way,
went on to demolish the Dolphins
by a score of 45 to 20, the Chargers
delighted to kick Miami's butt
up and down the truly grassy field.
The outcome left a huge doubt whether
the great coach Don Shula
would make the Playoffs or not.
What a shame that will be,
Frank allowed to Al and Dan,
both of whom agreed.

~ *November 1993*

# U.S. Dollars in El Salvador

A woman in El Salvador wanted to write a poem
about love, her dead husband
who was murdered by the military,
his slender legs, his lips,
his fiery eyes,
his callused loving hands
that knew the trails and secret places of her body,
but the woman's anger was a barking dog
that wouldn't leave her alone,
so she picked up her husband's gun,
and leaving her children,
walked into the dark green mountains
to where she needed to go.
There in the sanctuary of those mountains
she killed three soldiers in revenge
for the open wound of her husband's death.
The blood stained her hands.
Her anger then became a tree of sorrow.
She rooted herself in the mercy of those mountains,
and after a few years
she learned to dream about the animals—
monkeys, birds, jaguars, wild pigs,
even the same barking dog that had been her ferocious anger.
Those animals became her brothers and sisters.
They didn't have guns.
They lurked in the shadows.
They taught her lessons about innocence.

Together they waited for the wars to end.
The wars of course never ended.
The woman decided to stay in those mountains forever.
She decided that she would never write that poem about love.

*—October, 1990*

# The Lady with the Bugs on her Legs

The bugs on her beautiful legs were for scratching,
and so she called them her "scratch bugs."
She wore them everywhere she went.
In particular, she liked to wear them to the theater,
like the time she saw Kurosawa's unforgettable movie *Ran,*
and later to the elegant 3 a.m. coffeeshops.
She enjoyed sitting in a plush purple booth
next to the aisle and scratching at her bugs
which crawled from her ankles to her white thighs.
Since she was famous and beautiful too
many other women began to wear "scratch bugs,"
especially in San Francisco and Portland
where people seem to like animals and bugs more
than they do, say, in Indiana or Saint Louis, MO.
This phase of American fashion, of course,
did not last for long. She could have cared less.
She began wearing the bugs in her butch-cut hairdo,
she liked them to wander between her ample breasts
and down into the magic of her black pubic hair
where they became her "love bugs." The men of her life
understood, or at least they said they did,
but none stayed with her for long, not even Harry,
the multi-millionaire from Carmel who wore the bugs
himself for a week or so before he disappeared into the
tyranny of his wealth and she never heard from him again.
Still, she was undaunted. She had found the very
essence of her Self with her bugs and she could never

forgive herself if she relented from their favor.
She lived to the age of 73 after countless generations
of these bugs had passed over her body. As was her wish,
she was cremated, her faithful bugs asleep
in her brittle hair and the crevices of her cold body,
although a few, the undertaker said later,
escaped onto his arms and legs.
The next day, during a glorious red and pink sunset,
a few of her admirers rented an airplane
and scattered her ashes over the blue Pacific Ocean.

# Guatemala 1991

ANYONE TAKING an extra ration of food to their land plots could be accused of aiding the guerrillas and be shot.

Anyone caught taking extra clothes to their land plots, in case of rain, could be accused of aiding the guerrillas and be shot.

Anyone who was not at the flagpole at sundown every night, for roll call and a military lecture on the evils of communism, could be shot.

Anyone with a cache of extra medical supplies was in serious trouble with the base and could be shot.

Anyone who did not report any suspicious activities by a neighbor would be in serious trouble and could be shot or thrown off their lands.

Anyone who did not give twenty-four hours a week free guard duty to the civil patrols, as proof of his patriot fervor, could be called to the military base for questioning. The standard punishment was twenty-four hours of immersion in a pit filled with cold water.

Twenty-four hours a week of free civic duty was also expected and usually came in the form of making food for the soldiers, gathering firewood for the base, or clearing land around the trails to ensure safe passage for the military.

No one could leave the village without two permits—one from the base, and the one from the civil patrol leader.

After sundown, no one could leave the village at all.

*Who are the people who make these rules?*

They have names and they have mothers and fathers
They gouge out human eyeballs
They cut testicles off young boys
They stuff the testicles in the dead mouths
They rip the womb from pregnant women
They drink the good Guatemalan coffee
They eat black beans cooked with hamhock
They strangle their tortured victims
They rip out the fingernails
They touch the electric prod to a man's penis
They thrust it inside a woman
They feel sorrow and boredom
They burn hands and arms with cigarettes
They fuck the dead
They stick coke bottles into the womanhood of the dead
They drink whisky and smoke cigarettes
They burn the houses of the poor
They confiscate land
They buy good clothes and cars with their money
They make love with their beloved
In the dark nights they pray to God
They hang bloody bodies in the trees for the people to see
They kill the doctors and the priests
They decapitate the leaders of the enemy and impale their heads
They fear for their lives
Sometimes they sleep calmly in the warm and gentle nights

# Tury the Fag was Here

My name is Tury, and I'm from El Paso,
a feathery dry thing
that hovers cloud-like and dirty
in the fertile bed of my dreams.
If places can hate, then that's what
El Paso did, hated me,
flesh and bone, a bright red heart
that loved boys and men.
But El Paso is a good place to visit when you're dead.
Which is what I did.
I ate some gorditas over at Delicious,
I kissed my mother goodbye one last time,
and I said a little prayer
that was battered by the desert wind.
That's the best kind of prayer.
It gets lost and soiled
like me and everybody else.

> Dust to dust, I said.
> Blesséd be the dust.

Our Lady the Holiest was watching me.
Brown Lupita—
she understands love,
understands it comes from who you are.
She said: ¡Ya!
Ya está hecho.
She told me that my visit here was done,

and I was glad
because she promised me
that I could sleep forever in the arms of Jesus.


~ *in memory of Arturo Islas*

## Karma Finds Jesus Christ
## in El Paso

THE HOMELESS GUY with the prune head bought a twenty dollar money order with a 100 dollar bill, stuck the money order into an envelope and mailed it right there. Then he walked out of the downtown post office, stuffing his $80 of change into his money belt and talking to Jesus Christ over his right shoulder. He wanted Jesus to leave him alone, but Jesus was only telling him that he stunk to high and holy heaven. "You smell," Jesus said, "like the burros in Jerusalem." The homeless guy didn't understand. He turned around and told Jesus flat out he didn't care hammered-shit how he smelled as long as the horses were eating hay in Kentucky, and, by God, Jesus could put that in his pipe and smoke it.

Which is exactly what the Son of God did because the next time I saw Jesus, He was studying a racing form at the 7/11 down there at Cotton and Mesa Street. A black woman with big fat legs was telling Him what was what and stroking His precious thighs like there'd be no tomorrow.

"Tomorrows aren't in My line of work," Jesus said to her in a gentle and forgiving voice. She liked the way he sounded. "My name," she informed Him, "is Judy. What is it you care about, Honey?"

Jesus said in His deep baritone voice: "Really, all I care about is the fifth race at Sunland Park. There's a horse running named Eat Your Heart Out, Baby, and in that name rests all sorts of practical and mystical advice."

"Yeah?" Judy said, and she took Jesus home to her little upstairs apartment where they tried to live happily ever after. But that doesn't happen in the real world. One night some disenfranchised white supremacists, who had been black-balled and even erased from the membership rolls of the El Paso's lonely branch of the Klu Klux Klan, broke into the apartment and hung Jesus Christ from a tree. He forgave them, of course. But not Judy. The lady bought a Glock on the black market over in Juárez and went looking for them. Poor guys! Two weeks later Judy found them huddled up in their basement clubhouse in a mansion on top of Gato Loco Mountain.

# Winter Solstice, El Paso

Elvis was waiting for the downtown bus
at the corner of Piedras and Gold.
It was a cold and misty day, strange
dank weather for El Paso, a city
that gets maybe 11 inches of rain a year.
I knew it was Elvis because
when you see Elvis you know it's Elvis.
He was wearing a cowboy-cut brown suit
with a white shirt and a blue tie.
His gray hair was painted black and greasy.
I should have picked him up
and took him to the Rio Grande, opened the doors
into Mexico, the black velvet
paintings of him and John Lennon
sending desolate messages to Jesus Christ, but I didn't.
The short dark days make me too melancholy.
I stepped on the gas and disappeared,
wanting to leave well enough alone.
The bus behind me didn't stop either.

# June 17, 1993

IN LOS ALAMOS, in the Jemez Mountains of New Mexico, two nuclear physicists, Thomas Dowler and Joseph S. Howard, III, in fear of losing their precious jobs in the Post Cold War Era, have proposed designer nukes for our nuclear future:

> the ten-ton micro-nuke to destroy bunkers,
> the 100-ton mini-nuke to counter ballistic missiles,
> the 1000-ton tiny-nuke for battlefield attacks,
> and, finally, exotic technology warheads
> to do furious battle against various other threats.

Their proposal is documented in the paper, *Countering the Threat of the Well-Armed Tyrant, A Modest Proposal for Small Nuclear Warheads.* The two physicists, besides reminding their readers of Khomeini, Saddam Hussein, and others of like ilk, concluded their scientific, tactical and political arguments with a brief quotation from Robert Graves outlining the Orphic Creation Myth:

> The Orphics say that black-winged Night, a goddess of whom even Zeus stands in awe, was courted by the Wind and laid a silver egg in the womb of darkness; and that Eros, whom some call Phanes, was hatched from this egg and set the Universe in motion.

Nobody, of course, knew what the hell the two scientists meant by this quotation. That was their intent. The document, which has already made the rounds through the Pentagon and was initialed by General Colin Powell, Chairman of the Joint Chiefs of Staff, was forwarded through appropriate channels, to President Clinton's desk for further consideration.

## One of These Days
## Somebody Will Tell This Story

How one day
Hank Chinaski
famous drunken poet doppelganger
knocked at Charles Bukowski's door,

       knock knock
    knock knock.

"Hey, goddamnit, Buk, it's me!" he screamed.
Chinaski knew the old lady wasn't around,
had in fact
gone to do some shopping
at the Safeway and the liquor store,
the liquor store mostly.

                Anyway,
Bukowski opened the door and there was Chinaski,
his own concoction, Buk in the looking glass,
self-inflicted clone, ugly fucker,
staring him in the face.
What could he do?
What else do two drunks do?
They drank.
They drank wine,
two bottles of Mondavi Red.
"Good stuff, huh?" said the smart-ass Bukowski,
knowing of course it was better stuff

than Chinaski was used to.
"Yeah," snorted Chinaski.
He was peering at Bukowski's equally ugly face.
He hated looking at that face.

> Chinaski said: "I'm as ugly as you are."
> "Fuck you," said Bukowski.

They stared at each other some more.
Time passed dumbly like a fat horse in the 8th race
somewhere
in the middle of a hideously unlucky Saturday afternoon.
Chinaski knew it was his time to lay down his cards.
He was the guy who showed up at the door unwanted.
He was the guy who wanted to drive his junkheap into the hereafter
down whatever Los Angeles freeway that took him there.
He started talking about old times,
the bad times and the good,
the fuck-ass people and the booze.
Bukowski listened and drank.
Chinaski drank and talked.
Then Chinaski told Bukowski what he had come for.
He said he was tired of the goddamned doppelganger shit.
Bukowski mumbled: "What doppelganger shit?"
He smiled, he liked the word *doppelganger*.
Chinaski began shouting, he was leaning in close.
Bukowski could smell his stinking hot breath.
He screamed: "WELL, FUCK YOU!"
He jumped up, his fists cocked,
and he began to circle Hank Chinaski
like,
goddamnit,

now was the time to fight the real fight,
settle this business once and for all.

So here were these two old farts,
Charles Bukowski in his undershirt,
brown pants, and pink-ass shower thongs,
and Chinaski
in a moth-eaten wine-stained hand-me-down shirt,
identical drab-fucking brown pants,
and a idiotic pair of Italian loafers,
                              both of them writers and drunks,
        both of them
putting down their glasses of wine,
ready by God
to get down to the real work.
They circled and circled each other,
throwing flimsy 65-year-old left-handed jabs,
a rush here and there,
dodging back and forth.
Chinaski grabbed Bukowski by the undershirt,
pulled him into an old-man headlock,
and wrestled him to the floor.
They rolled around, kicked down a lamp,
knocked down one of the empties, splintering it into pieces.

        That's about it.
                Two minutes max.
                        End of fight.

Chinaski was able to get to his feet first.
Which made him the winner.
Bukowski understood. He screamed:

## "FUCK YOU, YOU BASTARD!
## GET OUT OF MY HOUSE!"

Chinaski, afloat in the harbor or his own rage,
kicked Bukowski in the groin
with those pointy-toed Italian shoes of his.
Bukowski groaned and wallowed around on the floor.
That was when Chinaski discovered he felt sorry for Bukowski.

"Oh, for Christ's sake, I'm sorry, Charley," he said.

Sorrow had indeed settled down in his heart
like a black crow at the dump.
He didn't like to be bothered by emotions.
They made him ordinary.
They made him hungry.
Bukowski, meanwhile, was on his back on the cold kitchen floor.
Black and white linoleum.
He stared up to see Hank Chinaski,
his own creation
with what looked like pity smeared across his pocked face.
That pissed Bukowski off.

"Fuck you," he said.
"I thought I told you to get the hell out of my house."

"Don't you want something to drink?"

"Of course I want something to drink."

Chinaski found a half bottle of vodka under the sink.
He poured them each a double.
"Here, take this," he growled.

"Never call me Charley, you motherless fucking bastard."

They both savored the irony of this curse.
Then they slugged the booze down like it was water.
But Chinaski still felt bad, bad because he kicked Buk.
He didn't come to kick Buk.
He wanted to get things straight.
He didn't want to be somebody else.
It was driving him nuts.
He wanted Buk to quit.
He wanted to get lost into nothing.
Like a library book on the wrong shelf.
The idea made good sense to him.
He put his glass down,
turned around and left the house,
slamming the door behind him.
He was mad and ashamed at himself,
because he wanted somehow
to give Bukowski a hug,
shake his hand,
something.
Didn't he,
for all those godforsaken years,
live inside the man's soul?
Or visa versa?
But Hank Chinaski couldn't do the one thing
that would free himself forever.
Instead, he walked down to his beatup Ford sedan
and drove away into the dirty city.
He lived in a cheap part of Hollywood,
a place that Bukowski had found,

close to the freeways and the racetrack,
a liquor store nearby.

Bukowski struggled to his feet,
cursing Chinaski,
cursing his own fucked up luck.
But he was curious too.
He wondered about the story of Chinaski,
how he could get this latest adventure into words.
Into a poem.
It sure wouldn't fit into a novel,
nothing like that would ever fit into a novel.
"Has to be the poem," Bukowski said out loud.
He reached to his mouth and nose
and felt the warm blood slowly dripping there.
"Oh, fuck," he said,
and stumbled over to where Chinaski had left the bottle.
He poured himself one more.

That afternoon the notorious writer,
Charles Bukowski,
checked into the hospital for tests.
The doctors found internal hemmoraging.
They asked him if he'd been in a fight.
Had he fallen down some stairs?
"Fuck you," Bukowski said.
"Fuck all doctors!
You're nothing but a bunch of soulless,
blood-fucking money-sucking assholes.
One day you'll all be trying to masturbate in Hell!

But there won't be nothing there, I tell you.
Your dick'll all be dried up.
Like dust in your fingers!
You jerks have no sense of what *real* really is."
And like many other times in his life,
Charles Bukowski was right.

# Gizmos

He gave her the glad eye.
She gave him the finger.

# Still The Heat Won't Go Away

It's been over 105 every day for a month now.
The pigeons are shitting on my front porch.
The flies won't go away.
"Wait for the rains," I tell my wife.
"Everything will be okay by the end of August."
My wife lies on the bed and refuses to listen.
She would consider a divorce, but it's too much trouble.
Meanwhile Our Lady of Guadalupe went back to Mexico.
She told a defrocked priest
that she couldn't stand the desert anymore, that
she wanted to feel the sweat dripping down
through the crevices of her body.
But really, it was the United States that was driving her nuts.
"The New World Order is worse than Christianity,"
she told Jesus Christ, her serene confidante,
who was waiting for her
outside JC Penny's at the Sunland Park Mall,
his suitcase packed and ready to go.
Judas was driving the car.
Now the three of them are making ends meet
selling ice cream and paletas in Tepic.
I know because they sent me
a pretty picture postcard,
the heads of three green parrots
cocked like pistols.

"We are innocent," Judas writes.
"Innocence is the essence of our nature.

Every day our Lupita takes a bath,
she sleeps in a bed of white and pink flowers.
Chuy drinks Bohemia beer and Dos Equis,
las claras o las oscuras, He doesn't care which,
He eats the mangos by the dozen, He enjoys
the taste of barbecued fish covered
with cilantro and the juice of the lime.
The three of us take turns killing the bugs."

Like always, Judas closed his remarks
by reminding us
that the end of the world is always near.
That's his job.
He sends his love.

# The Handsome Stranger

A dark stranger in the fancy Mexican hat
strolled like one of Diego Rivera's
héroes de la Revolución
on a Sunday afternoon in the Alameda
into my neighbor's backyard
where a pit bull was barking
and yelping away his sorrows.
The handsome stranger crossed himself
and spit into the afternoon dust.
An old-fashioned silvery gun
slipped into his strong right hand
like a six-petaled flower, blooming—

BANG

BANG

and the door slammed shut
on that poor dog's life.
Sure, the dog squirmed a bit
in its complete surprise,
blood leaking out of its
gigantic pit bull grin.
Speaking very slowly
so even I could understand
his sweet-smelling Spanish,
the man told me that nobody
should let a dog live like that,
chained up in the radiance

of a hot desert day,
no water, no food, nothing.
"I don't think the dog
even had a name," he said.
The handsome stranger scowled at me:
"Where in the hell have you been?
Can't you even love a dog?"
Then he walked away,
the barrel of his muscular
six-shooter smoking
hot creamy juices
like the sweet milk
from the Virgin's breast.

# A Clown Talks About
# My Mother's Soul

LIKE A LOT OF OTHER CLOWNS, this guy had a big red bulbous nose and curly orange hair, but he wore a gray double-breasted business suit with a red silk Jerry Garcia tie and a matching hanky that stuck gaudily out of his lapel pocket.

He even had on a $200 pair of black Florsheim wingtips.

I didn't know what to make of him, especially after he decided to lecture me about my 80-year-old mother.

Her soul, he said, is part of the genetic structure of God. It's the way the universe works, and he drew a picture of my mother's soul on the sidewalk. He was careful to use all of the 64 colors in a large box of Crayolas. Still, in those two dimensions the drawing seemed like nothing more than glittering graffiti tattooed against a field of empty space, but he said that in the sixth dimension the soul becomes a drop of luminous nectar swollen with memory of the holy.

It's just like yours, yours and mine too, he said, a twisted lipsticked smile cracking his chalky face. And don't forget your little sister Patty who tumbled down the stairs into the fat homey life of perfect mystery. We are all essential elements in the business of naming God.

Me and this clown were both silent for a while.

I wanted to ask him some questions—what was his name? where did he come from? how did he learn all of his information?—but I didn't.

I just kept quiet like I always do.

I did want to cry, but his cheeky manner insinuated that he would have none of that. He clapped his white-gloved hands and did a sad-faced little jig that mocked me, but also made me glad that he decided to talk to me and show me these things. Then he offered to buy me a cup of cappuccino or expresso at La Dolce Vita over on Cincinnati Street. He said he particularly likes the large cup of their French Roast with just a dash of real cream and a little bit of cinnamon.

# The Gabachos in the Photograph

They'll tell you when you're growing up
that water goes under the bridge,
but they don't tell you about the bridge
that goes over to Avenida Juárez
where Martino's Restaurant is
two doors down from the Kentucky Club.
The imagination opens those doors,
and there I am,
the big bearded gabacho in the straw hat,
the coral necklace,
drinking Dos XX Oscura
and thinking I will have enough riches in my pocket
to nourish my heart in case of love.
It's Lee's 32nd birthday, 1977,
a year before we moved to El Paso.
Isn't she beautiful?
I am 35.
We sit in the corner booth by the windows
where the tiny Tarahumara children stand forever
with their outstretched hands
reaching into the emptiness of the 20th Century,
and a kaleidescope of people walk
back and forth
looking for ways to lose themselves
in the dwindling twilight.
Glittering mirrors.
Hard-crusted bolillo rolls.
French onion soup.

Chateaubriand for two fried in butter French-style.
We become stuffed and drunk and happy.
We wander the streets holding hands,
we climb a rickety staircase
to a small $10 room with clean sheets,
we make love like resplendent wild beasts
in search of something Jesus said,
and then we walk back into
the jingle-jangle of Avenida Juárez.

That was twenty-one years ago now.
Nothing has really changed except us.
Pedro Ruelas Alvarez,
the street photographer who took this picture
is dead now.
Like my mother is dead.
My sister Patsy.
My brother Bill.
Like Lee's mother and father.

"Water under the bridge, ¿verdad?"

Another gabacho couple is sitting in that booth tonight.
They are looking out the window
at the Indian children with the large black eyes,
and they are afraid
of what they see in that confusion.
Give them a quarter, mister,
give them a dollar,
give them back the secret places
in the mountains where their spirit thrives.

That's what I always want to do,
to give away something to make myself whole,
but it seems so impossible,
even to give something to myself.
At least I feel like I am at home now,
here in El Paso,
walking back and forth across the bridge,
and I'm hoping to find enough riches in my pocket
to cure some of the ache in my heart.
This is my prayer—
May God grant us all love
and a little bit of peace on Avenida Juárez.
Amen.

# Goodbye

Ricardo took a look at his body
withered and yellow
cancerous rot
worthless loins
stench of hospital
reduced he was to perfection
his very self
Teresa entering the room

ding

        ding

                ding

angel cloth damp and cool
the desert light like shine
on the side of a 1969 Impala
a .357 Magnum oiled
a silver dollar
watermelons
manstuff
Mexicans crossing the river
the eyeball of God
who it turned out
for the pure exercise
was a one-eyed woman
lived in one of those
roach infested apartments
off Paisano
did some curandera work

## Ricardo Sánchez

who always wanted to believe
thought for a few seconds

said in English
Fuck this
and he meant every word of it
so slipped he away
yesterday
Sunday the Lord's Day
September 3 1995
carried with himself into the darkness
the sweet smell of Teresa
those beautiful eyes
a snapshot of his kids grandkids
toda la familia
some jingle jangle for the santos
anillos pesados for every finger of the holiness Our Lady
tiny black spot of rage that clung to his soul
a 1000 or so words in spanish
ditto the english
the lingo inbetween
una mezclada de syntactical secrets
the como se llama of poverty
freshly devised manifestos re: the democracy of divinity
a couple of useless names of friends to throw at the wind
neon blue pen red satin handkerchief
manual typewriter white paper a notebook
some crayons for Manny
garlic onions beans

right rear haunch of northern new mexico venison
fresh mesilla valley tomatoes
tortillas de maiz de méxico
the best bottle of tequila he could find
un cóctel molotov para buena suerte
organic coffee picked by communists
absolutely no money
curious grin
a fist
no
two fists
made of soft chicano hands
various hunks of silver jewelry turquoise red beaded necklace
etcetera

naked as the day he was born

emerged like that funny looking Indian saint

with a pack on his back

the bato stopped by my house

played a little tune on a penny whistle

and said goodbye .

## In Paradise

Franz Kafka lies in the brittle arms of Gregor Samsa.
Gregor is fairly happy, but Franz—he's not sure.

# Dream of a Sunday Afternoon in La Alameda Central

*Mexico City / July 1994*
*∼ for Joe Hayes*

Blas, your favorite waiter,
the handsome Indian-looking man
with the broad smile,
serves you a capuchino
at El Trevi,
a good but inexpensive restaurant

        which today
    seems
to be a pretty good answer

to the question of existence,
especially if you, like me
(a gringo, an improvisational wanderer
of Mexico City streets),
have completed the obligatory
Sunday evening promenade
back and forth
through the crowded walks
and tall dark trees
of La Alameda Central.

                If so,
you've seen and meditated on

the man with the two boa constrictors
and his team of conspirators
who were selling guaranteed remedies

> for sexual impotency,
> for the sudden heart attack
> that killed your father,
> for varicose veins,
> for the upset stomach,
> for life itself,

and you believed every word he said
because you have rubbed elbows with poor people,
rich people and people in-between,
and in the midst of their bodies you caught
the faint whiff of all the meanings of love.
It was there, suddenly,
in the twilight
sometime after six in the midst
of the history of Mexico,

> there

> tangled
> among

the sweethearts stealing kisses on the park benches,
the babies huddled in their mothers' arms, that
peculiar old man walking his dog with the dangling broken leg,
the middle-aged couple strolling hand-in-hand
having just forgiven each other all their many sins,

> there

in the shrill voices of vendors hustling a living,
the money changing hands, there even
in the refrescos fríos, the helados y paletas,
melones, papayas, mangos,
tacos ricos de todo tipo de guisados,
images of the Baby Jesus, images
of Jesus Christ truly suffering on the Cross,
Nuestra Señora de Guadalupe blessing us all,
color fotos of grandma and grandpa,
the belts, nail clippers, scotch tape, shampoo,
pens and pencils, Chiclets, newspapers and magazines,
a pair of shiny black shoes, size 12,
everything that you may possibly need
to live and die with
on a crowded Sunday afternoon
walking alone in the dream of
La Alameda Central.

                But now you've made your promenade,
           and you're sitting at a table

just like any other customer
who enjoys the absolute white
of a table cloth at El Trevi.
Blas with the broad smile
is serving you the capuchino in a glass
with a dash of cinnamon
floating on top the fluffy cream.
The people are still walking by the window.

        Life never quits,
           Blas whispers to you

in Spanish,

and he says that it's okay if you die
in the morning maybe,
or next year, or whenever.
What difference would it truly make?
Isn't Diego dead, he asks?
And your friends Mike and Jimmy and David?
And Gail Brandon too?
                              You stir the capuchino
until the coffee, the steamed milk,
the cinnamon, the spoon,
the muscle and bone of your fingers and wrist—

they all become one thing
perfectly.
Maybe you add a little sugar.
Still, the capuchino is too hot.
You must wait.
In the waiting you get lost in your self
and you forget about Blas,
         but that's okay,
              that's part of the dream.

## You are the Reason
## I Came Home
## from Mexico City

It's late Saturday night
I'm on the front porch drinking wine
And eating delicious summer watermelon
Spitting the black seeds up under the grape trellises
You're already asleep
Sleeping a virtuous sleep
Because you're wiser than me
I know that
Sometimes that makes me mad
But tonight I'm happy
Just to be wondering if those few stars
That are hanging south of the Rio Grande
Are Aries
Or maybe they're Gemini
I never could remember the constellations
One month to the next
But that's okay because tonight
I decide to invent my own cosmology
And there we are
Me and you together in some sort of celestial mystery novel
You're in hard trouble with the Law
Darkness and Chaos surround you
They are playing on the same team forever
God is not paying attention
All the Angels are speaking Spanish

You decide to come to me instead of looking around
in the Yellow Pages for Sam Spade or Jesus Christ
You ask me questions about the meanings of life and death
But I can only shake my head
To make you understand that I don't know
You smile at my honesty
I smile at your innocence
We fall in love again
Life gets complicated and we escape into the Milky Way
We have a close scrape with death
Some handsome thug is carrying a gun but I shoot him full of
Walt Whitman
He enjoys my anger
He apologizes like a fish feasting on pomegranates
He begs my forgiveness
I let him go
He says his name is Maximo Arroyo
Anytime I need a favor, just give him a call
And he walks away into the helter-skelter of the starry night
O yes I almost forgot
On the radio salsa de caribe is banging away
Johnny Pacheco struts the pachanga
He makes me shake my hips

Chup-chup-bu-ra
Buu-ra
Buu-ra
Chunga-chunga-chang

*O my love, the night is full of sorrow*

Chup-chup-bu-ra
Buu-ra
Buu-ra
Chunga-chunga-chang

*O my love, the earth is fierce*

Chup-chup-bu-ra
Buu-ra
Buu-ra
Chunga-chunga-chang

*O my love, our souls want to carouse in the delicate void*

Chup-chup-bu-ra
Buu-ra
Buu-ra
Chunga-chunga-chang

*O my love, I am dancing the long dark night with you*

# It's My Turn to Clean Up the Dogshit in the Backyard

IT'S WINTER SOLSTICE, and for three days now it's either been snow or rain, thick heavy clouds hanging on the Franklin Mountains that wouldn't let go, so the ground's still damp and cold. El Paso's not supposed to be like this. This is the Chihuahua Desert. This is the border between Mexico and the United States. Too much darkness and people get depressed, they get drunk, shoot their wives, shoot their husbands, shoot themselves.

So it was good when last night I saw the full moon breaking through the clouds. It was Tuesday night, my basketball night. I'd drank too many beers with my friends at the L&J, and I was driving home over the mountain. The city lights were sparkling, the moon aglow with my drunkenness, but I felt lonely. They're good guys, my friends, all of them, but they don't like poetry. It would have been nice to talk to somebody like Li Po or Pablo Neruda, William Carlos Williams, maybe my dead friend Paul Blackburn, any of my heroes who walk in Heaven among the Angels, somebody who would understand, do you know what I mean?

Can you imagine?

Me and these dead poets are huddled up in the corner of the L&J Bar, talking about real and important things, smoking Camel cigarettes and drinking beer from a pitcher. I bring up the Buddhist concept of Nothingness, of breathing in and out, how all things must change, how all beings must suffer and die. Li Po sighs and fills our glasses full again with beer. He wishes that I would shut up. It would be better, he says, that I tell him about the woman across the room.

Why is she alone, he wonders?

I tell him I don't know. Her name is Ruth. Her red hair is all I know about her.

That is all we need to know, says Bill Williams as he looks over his shoulder at the woman and studies her in his doctor sort of way.

Pablo laughs and tells a story about a red-headed woman he met once, in a bar like this one, how she saved his life when he was crossing the Andes to safety. The Army wanted him dead. He was a poet. He was a communist. On the very top of a mountain pass on a bitterly cold day, the federales catching up quick, the red-headed woman made love to him under a pile of blankets. Her nipples, Pablo said, were like red berries. Sweet and warm red berries.

Paul giggles and pulls at his scraggly goatee. He is so delighted to be among the living again with a glass of cold beer cupped in his hands. He decides to say a few lines from one of the ancient Provençal poets—

> *I shall make a verse about*
> *nothing,*
> *downright nothing, not*
> *about myself or youth or love*
> *or anyone.*
> *I wrote it on horseback dead asleep*
> *while riding in the sun.*

The poets cheer, especially Neruda who has a big-lipped grin wrapped across his face. He says he's delighted that the Europeans have this large place in their past where they can go looking for *duende*. Bill Williams has a grin too, but his grin seems still to be wrapped around the thighs of the mujer with the nipples like red berries. Li Po, who turns out oddly enough to be quite a loquacious drunk, elbows the good doctor and offers a toast to the Café of Death.

The Café of Death? I ask.

Paul shushes me while Li Po clears his throat and proclaims in a loud voice, To the Café of Death! The assemblage of dead poets raise their glasses to the Café of Death. They drink and nod their heads because they understand what I do not understand. Paul looks at me with his sparkling eyes. I will have plenty of time to understand, he says.

I say, Yeah, I guess I will.

Meanwhile, two tables over my basketball friends sit in their stinking sweats and drink their beers, laughing and hooting at my poet friends and me. Like I said, they don't give a rat's ass about poetry, but they know I got other wishes too. They know I wish I wasn't 55 years old and overweight, they know I wish I didn't drink so much, they know I wish that I could hit a jump shot from 15 feet out.

## Yellow Flowers in the Spring

The trouble with daffodils, she said, is that they die.

# Memo to
# My Granddaughter Hannah

Rufus the Cat is chasing his tail.
Which means
the Holy Ghost is chasing the Holy Ghost.
Like you are two years old, your mother
is my daughter, and
my own mother is dead now.
She was the Holy Ghost dying.
The rattle in her throat,
her parched lips,
pale blue eyes,
all those last few days a message
to the beginning and to the end
to the up and to the down
to the dark and to the light
saying goodbye.
I held her hand while she died.

## 15 Minutes.

Sit. Count my breaths. Wind
chimes announce nothing. Mother
is dead. Alarm rings.

# Notes and Acknowledgements

Otto Campbell, and a group of cholos that he recruited from the streets of Juárez, painted the mural *La Brigada por la Paz* which is the central image of the cover's photograph. Campbell was a Mexican artist and political activist who died in 1997 soon before his 68th birthday. Mexican novelist Willivaldo Delgadillo says of Campbell, "He had a man-size wisdom and was one of those rare human beings who appeared to be reconciled with himself." The mural was painted on the corner of a major intersection in Juárez—Avenida Diez y Seis de Septiembre and Avenida Francisco Villa—which is right across the street from el restaurante Villa del Mar. I was having lunch with Joe Somoza there the only time that I had the opportunity to see it. Soon afterwards it was obliterated. Again, Willivaldo: "The local Coca-Cola honcho ordered it removed because he didn't like the fact that the bishop had a $-sign on his hat. The mural was replaced by a small notice on the newly painted wall that reads: *Please Do Not Advertise. Coca-Cola.*"

The cover photograph is by Virgil Hancock of Tucson, Arizona. It appears in a remarkable collection of his photographs, *Chihuahua, Pictures from the Edge* (University of New Mexico Press, 1966, with a companion essay by Charles Bowden). Cinco Puntos thanks him whole-heartedly.

The charcoal drawing that faces the title page, and is repeated again at the end of the book, is by David Nakabayashi of El Paso. David is one of those paseño artists who is hounded by friends telling him to move to "where something is happening," meaning places like Santa Fe, Los Angeles, et cetera. He never does because there is always something happening for him. He used the poem "The Price of Doing Business in Mexico" as source for this drawing.

In the poem "The Price of Doing Business in Mexico," I named the second waiter Rafa Guillén because that is supposedly the real name— as alleged by Ernesto Zedillo and the Mexican government—of subcomandante Marcos, the most visible of the leaders of the Zapatista rebels in Chiapas. Whether or not the Rafa Guillén of my poem is truly Marcos, I don't know. The Hotel San Francisco is, sadly enough, a very real place in Toluca.

James Evans, a freelance photographer who lives in Marathon, TX, took the photograph of the man in the "ghilli" suit, the camouflaged outfit worn by the U.S. Marines who shot and killed Esequiel Hernández, Jr. After the death of Esequiel, James was asking around to see if anybody had a ghilli suit, and a local rancher came forward with one that the marines had left on his land. The man inside the suit is Mike Howard, an assistant to Evans. The photograph originally appeared in *The Texas Monthly* (August, 1997) as illustration to an article entitled "Soldiers of Misfortune" by Robert Draper. I highly recommend this article for anyone wishing to learn more of that tragic event.

The title of the poem "Dream of a Sunday Afternoon in La Alameda Central" is the English translation of the title of Diego Rivera's mural, *Sueño de una Tarde Dominical en la Alameda Central*. In the mural Diego is a child who stands in the Alameda among the constellation of his personal heroes (his lover and colleague Frida Kahlo, the artist Posada, et cetera), the good guys and bad guys of the Mexican Revolution, and a female calaca—a skeleton who is, of course, Death. After the earthquake in Mexico City, the mural was moved from the crumbling hotel where it was originally created to a small museum a block from the Alameda and two doors down from el restaurante Trevi. El Trevi, by the way, is an excellent place to enjoy an inexpensive comida while watching the perambulations of pedestrians outside the huge plate glass windows.

Ricardo Sánchez (1942–1995), for whom the elegy "Goodbye" was written, was the proto-typical pachuco poet. Cantankerous, eloquent and passionate, he issued from a community tradition of oral poetry which in Spanish is known as "declamación." I have always found it interesting that there is no synonym for that word in English.

In the poem "The Gabachos in the Photograph," the word "gabacho" is a synonym for "gringo" but perhaps not with such a pejorative taste. Pedro Ruelas Alvarez, the street photographer who took the photograph of Lee and I, died sometime in the early 1990s. Martino's is a wonderful restaurant. Many of the equally wonderful waiters— including my favorite, Moisés II, a dead-ringer for Peter Lorre—have been working there for decades. They all make exquisite martinis right at your table while you sit and watch.

Richard Baron took the photograph of me which is on the back cover flap. In the 1980s he had done a series entitled "Border Retratos" of men in downtown El Paso. I had always admired those photographs because they seemed to catch the true nature of the desert light and the way it reveals a person's face. The hat is my favorite from the El Paso Diablos (Double-A ball, Texas League).

Several poems in this collection were written, or initially conceived, when I was living in Mexico City in 1994 as a fellow in the International Program of the National Endowment for the Arts. This cultural exchange program was funded jointly by the NEA and Las Belles Artes de México. It has since been dismantled because of lack of funding.

The poems listed below appeared, in slightly different versions, in a fine hand-made, letter press edition with illustrations by David McLimans. That book, entitled *Art in America*, was produced by typographer, bookmaker and artist Walter Hamady for his Perishable Press. Poems included in that collection are "The Price of Doing Business in Mexico," "Whatever Happened to Art in America?" under a different title, "Dream of a Sunday Afternoon in La Alameda Central," and "July in the Desert of Chihuahua." Persons interested in Perishable Press books may contact Walter at 201 Jeglum Valley Road; Mt. Horeb, WI 53572–3200. Other poems have been published by *Puerto del Sol, Sin Fronteras, Rio Grande Review* and *Blue Mesa* Review. It is quite possible that, because of my chaotic record keeping, that I am neglecting to mention magazines where some of these poems have first appeared. If so, my apologies to the editors.

There are many thanks that must go along with the publication of this book. First, to Janine Pommy Vega, Joe Somoza, Rus Bradburd, Diane Wakoski and Lee Merrill Byrd for their careful reading of these poems while in manuscript, and for their suggestions and encouragement. To Willivaldo Delgadillo and David Romo for their help with the Spanish phrasing that I have used in some of the poems. To Steve Yellen for being purely Steve Yellen. To Susannah Byrd and John Byrd for prodding their old man along in his career as a poet, surely an odd concept for any child to grasp, as their younger brother Andy will testify. To Edward Holland for providing me with the extra time I've always wanted and needed to go about the business of my poetry. Finally, to Vicki Trego Hill, the designer and typographer for this book. She too reads carefully my poems, and as the book progressed, it changed to the better because of her editorial ear and artistic eye.

# Recent Cinco Puntos Press Books from the Border and from Mexico

*Tonatiuh's People,*
*A Novel of the Mexican Cataclysm,*
by John Ross

*Dirty Dealing, Drug Smuggling on the Mexican Border*
*and the Assassination of a Federal Judge—An American Parable,*
non-fiction by Gary Cartwright.

*Ghost Sickness,*
Poems by Luis Alberto Urrea

*Modelo Antiguo, A Novel of Mexico City,*
by Luis Eduardo Reyes,
(translated by Sharon Franco and Joe Hayes)

*The Moon Will Forever Be a Distant Love,*
a novel by Luis Humberto Crosthwaite,
(translated by Debbie Nathan and Willivaldo Delgadillo)

*The Late Great Mexican Border, Reports from a Disappearing Line,*
a collection of essays from prominent writers
with unique perspectives about the region,
edited by Bobby Byrd and Susannah Mississippi Byrd

*Dark and Perfect Angels,*
poems by Benjamin Alire Sáenz

*For more information or a catalog contact:*

**CINCO PUNTOS PRESS**
**2709 Louisville**
**El Paso, TX 79930**
**1-800-566-9072**